Silly Sally

by Audrey Wood

Harcourt, Inc.

ORLANDO   AUSTIN   NEW YORK   SAN DIEGO   TORONTO   LONDON

Requests for permission to make copies of any part of the work should be mailed to the following address: Permissions Department, Harcourt, Inc., 6277 Sea Harbor Drive, Orlando, Florida 32887-6777.

Wood, Audrey.
Silly Sally/by Audrey Wood.
p.   cm.
Summary: A rhyming story of Silly Sally, who makes many friends as she travels to town—backwards and upside down.
ISBN 0-15-274428-2
[1. Humorous Stories.   2. Stories in rhyme.]   I. Title.
PZ8.3.W848Si   1992
[E]—dc20   91-15939

TWP   31 30 29 28 27 26
4500220724

The paintings in this book were done in Winsor & Newton watercolors on Arches watercolor paper.
The display type was hand lettered by the illustrator, based on a rendering by Brenda Walton, Sacramento, California.
The text type was set in Adroit Light by Thompson Type, San Diego, California.
Color separations by Bright Arts, Ltd., Singapore
Printed and bound by Tien Wah Press, Singapore
This book was printed on totally chlorine-free Stora Enso Matte paper.
Production supervision by Warren Wallerstein and Ginger Boyer
Designed by Michael Farmer

Printed in Singapore

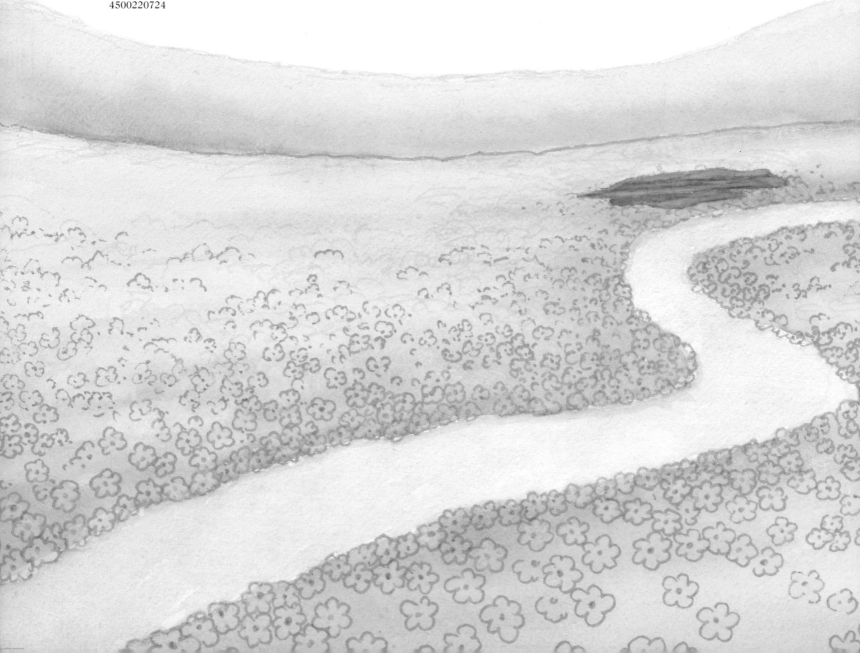

For Ann and Warren Wallerstein

Silly Sally went to town,
walking backwards, upside down.

On the way she met a pig,
a silly pig,

they danced a jig.

Silly Sally went to town,
dancing backwards, upside down.

On the way she met a dog,
a silly dog,

they played leapfrog.

Silly Sally went to town,
leaping backwards, upside down.

On the way she met a loon,
a silly loon,

they sang a tune.

Silly Sally went to town,
singing backwards, upside down.

On the way she met a sheep,
a silly sheep,

they fell asleep.

Now how did Sally get to town,
sleeping backwards, upside down?

Along came Neddy Buttercup,
walking forwards, right side up.

He tickled the pig
who danced a jig.

He tickled the dog
who played leapfrog.

He tickled the loon
who sang a tune.

He tickled the sheep
who fell asleep.

He tickled Sally,
who woke right up.

She tickled Neddy Buttercup.

And that's how Sally got to town,

walking backwards, upside down.